Figures in Blue

Books by Ted Morrissey

An Untimely Frost, a novel
Men of Winter, a novel
The Beowulf *Poet and His Real Monsters*, a monograph

Figures in Blue

A Novelette

Ted Morrissey

Twelve Winters Press

Sherman, Illinois

Published by

Twelve Winters Press, LLC

P. O. Box 414
Sherman, IL 62684-0414

TwelveWinters.com • xii.winters@gmail.com

The print edition of *Figures in Blue* was first published by Twelve Winters Press in 2013. The electronic edition of *Figures in Blue* was first published by Battered Suitcase Press in 2013.

Cover & Interior Page Design: Ted Morrissey
Cover Art: *Blue Girl* copyright © Felicia Olin
Author Photo: copyright © Shannon O'Brien

ISBN
978-0-9895151-3-9

Printed in the United States of America

For the Master, William H. Gass
& the artists of The Pharmacy

Acknowledgments

Figures in Blue has been published as an e-novelette by Battered Suitcase Press, a division of Vagabondage Press. Over the last couple of years I've spent a significant amount of time at The Pharmacy art center in Springfield, Illinois, and I'm certain that my time there, communing with the artists and their works of art, especially their works in progress, was a great source of inspiration for this story. I would like to thank Pamm Collebrusco for her expert editing and proofreading; and Felicia Olin for her generosity in allowing me to use *Blue Girl* for the cover illustration.

A Note on the Cover

Blue Girl, 24 x 36 inches, oil on masonite, 2012, is by the Springfield-based artist Felicia Olin, who's work has been shown throughout Illinois, including in solo shows in Chicago galleries. She is one of the founding members of The Pharmacy art center in Springfield. On her website she writes, "I've always been met with love and appreciation for what I do. It makes me truly content to fill the world with images I find beautiful, and to find an audience that shares that vision." For more about Felicia and her work visit the following:

feliciaolin.com
flea-sha.deviantart.com
thepharmacygallery.com

Figures in Blue

No one who is thrust into the den of
the Minotaur ever comes out again.

—James Baldwin, *Old Greek Stories*

1

FROM THE VILLAGE STREETS BELOW, THE HOUSE DID APPEAR
magnificent, with its towers and leaded glass and Cyprium roof
of verdant patina—truly baronial and hence ideally suited for
the dowager baroness, Kristena von Lichtenberg—but as the
young painter made his way along the upward-winding flagstone path he began to see the disrepair that had come to the
house and grounds, like unwelcome dispatches from an army
which is slowly but inevitably losing the war. He was lugging
the leather portfolio case that held a sketchbook, charcoal pencils, and examples of his work, though only three studies of por-
traiture as it had never been his primary interest. He preferred
bodies in motion, thus painting mainly from imagination. He
believed that each single moment of, for instance, a gypsy's
dance was imprinted indelibly somewhere in one's mind, like
a piece in an enormous gallery, and he had only to conjure that
moment with his brushes and blades . . . but the trick was locat-
ing the correct gallery salon.

At last he came to the portico and looked up at the underside of its roof, which showed the mold-colored water stains of
years of leaking rain and snowmelt. Each stain was picketed by
large flakes of mauve paint which shook steadily but soundless-
ly in a persistent breeze that couldn't be felt in the village streets
below. The young painter, Esteban, had begun to perspire from
the strain of carrying the portfolio case up the steep path, and
he stood for a moment enjoying the cooling breeze.

Esteban had been in the village more than six months but
it was only supposed to be a brief stopover, to rest and perhaps
earn a few marks, before continuing his journey to the Rhine
Valley, where his master and the other artists in the Sevillean

colony claimed that the light was crafted by God Himself, intended only to illuminate heaven . . . however, the valley was so close to being heaven, they said, the Divine One had made an exception.

That had been the plan at least—was still the plan—but Esteban quickly found work in the village stables (he was well accustomed to horses) and he also discovered that the light here bewitched him. Instead of the ruddy golden hue of the Rhine light, as the old artists had said and as he'd observed in their masterworks, the light here was infused with indigo, as if the sky had become lonely and rode the sunlight down to earth, beam upon beam, to be among living creatures. But the fellowship made no difference and the deep blue of the light retained its air of isolation, of melancholy. It was a lugubrious illumination but it touched Esteban's soul . . . and days turned to weeks, weeks to months. . . .

He went to the twin oaken doors and reached for the brass knocker fashioned in the shape of a pointed-edged sun, so disused that filaments of cobwebs ran between the points, but he'd only touched the cold metal when the door opened freely and an envelope fell to the stone floor. He saw his name written in spidery, feminine script—*Herr Espíritu*—and he picked up the rose-tinged envelope, which he realized immediately was expensive stationery. As he opened the unsealed envelope he smelled the subtle fragrance of rose. He unfolded the letter, also of the blushing stationery, with the baroness's family seal embossed at the head, and read in the same thin, looping handwriting, *Please, come to the conservatory, Herr Espíritu, at the rear of the house—K.L.* His German was not yet fluent, especially this provincial dialect, but he believed he understood the note.

Esteban replaced the letter to the envelope and put it in his jacket's side pocket. He'd worn his olive corduroy jacket, blue cotton shirt, and coarse canvas trousers—the best clothes that he owned but still shabby for the interview, he felt. He set foot upon the entryway's parquet floor, rosewood, and thought of the heel of his left boot which had started to come loose, though it wasn't obvious at a glance.

The inside of the house was not in as severe a state of disrepair as the outside but it was clear that the baroness was without a full staff. In fact no one at all stirred at Esteban's entrance, and he detected not a soul in the house—not so much as a sleepy cat.

As he walked along the central hallway, with various rooms open to either side, Esteban realized that the same sapphire light he associated with the valley itself permeated this space as well, even though the few windows he saw were curtained—however, only by a sheer panel of simple white lace, that is to say, dingy white lace as they likely hadn't been properly taken down and laundered for years.

His eyes were becoming used to the subdued lighting, so when he finally entered the conservatory, which at first appeared entirely constructed of glass, Esteban had to squint against the relative brightness, and it took him a moment to locate the source of the greeting he heard:

Ah, there you are, Herr Espíritu—thank you so much for accepting my invitation. The baroness was seated in an ornately carved chair of crimson velvet and wood so dark it was nearly ebon. She wore a gown of Oriental blue silk and white lace. Her hair was pure white and long enough to be braided and looped back over her shoulder—a style he'd only seen maidens wearing, yet it seemed to suit her. The baroness was thin but not frail-looking. His impression was that she was tall for a woman. In addition to several pieces of furniture, the conservatory was home to numerous large-leafed plants, and the baroness in her chair was all but concealed by potted foliage. He was reminded of a Goya etching of Eden.

Yes, he said, I am pleased to oblige you.

The baroness smiled, at his awkward phrasing, he suspected, and he hoped that his tanned face was not revealing a blush. He had had a beard of several days' growth but shaved himself clean for the interview. The gruff-looking fellow who came to Esteban's boardinghouse room, wearing a suit of clothes too small for his wide frame, said only that the baroness Kristena wished to see him about painting her portrait. Esteban had had steady work in the stables—in Seville he trained mounts for use in the bullring so tending to the village's workaday horses was nothing—but still time and space for his art had suffered, thus the idea of a patroness very much appealed to his ambitions. Seeing the condition of the baroness's house and grounds, however, had cooled his hopes. Nevertheless he was curious as to what she had in mind, and even a modestly paying project was better than no project at all.

Won't you have a seat; looking up pains my neck. She first motioned toward another velvet-covered chair, also ornately carved, yet not a twin to her own as its wood was lightly stained—then she brought her hand to her neck, merely touching it through her high lace collar. Esteban noted that while her face retained a youthful radiance, in spite of its many fine wrinkles, her hands were typically those of an old woman: almost skeletal in their thinness with the blue of her veins easily projecting through the rice-paper skin, and swollen knuckle joints that stood out like undersized walnuts.

Would you care for some chocolate? Though it is no longer especially hot. She nodded toward a silver serving pot on a small table within Esteban's reach, and a cup and saucer of delicate and diminutive design. Esteban had found German chocolate to be quite bland compared to the chocolate shops of Seville but his long walk had drained him a bit, so he thanked the baroness and helped himself.

She waited to speak until after he had taken a sip of the chocolate, which was more to his taste than he had anticipated.

It is very good, he said, thank you. The German still felt quite alien on his tongue.

How have you been enjoying our little village, Herr Espíritu?

It is . . . restful.

She smiled, revealing straight teeth whose whiteness was only partially dulled by age. Yes, I imagine for a young man, a young Spaniard no less, our village seems quite sleepy.

Esteban flinched inwardly at the insinuation that all Spanish men were hot-blooded, that their nature rejected an introspective life, but he let the remark pass unchallenged. He drank more chocolate, becoming accustomed to its milky taste.

I believe Franz explained why I wanted to see you.

Oh yes—Esteban placed his cup and saucer on the table, undid the leather ties of his portfolio case, and removed the samples of his work, perhaps all a bit too eagerly—and he handed them to the baroness.

In truth, he said, I have not done many portraits, as you see—but I am interested in the form. (He heard the falseness in his words and the clarity of their real meaning: but I am interested in accepting your money.)

The baroness's fingers were arthritically clumsy and it took her a few moments to examine the pieces. Esteban sipped at his chocolate while watching her face closely, in particular the lines around her eyes of raven blue: the expression remained one of curiosity with no sign of judgment: she may have loved his work or despised it.

She let the art rest on her lap; the piece on top was a chalk drawing of a gypsy girl, no older than sixteen or seventeen, who has retrieved water from the village well and is observing her reflection in the pail with subtle but obvious satisfaction. Esteban was especially pleased with the drawing.

I see, said the baroness, that the reports are true: you are a young man of talent.

Thank you—wondering about the source of the baroness's information.

You seem ideally suited to render the sort of portrait I have in mind.

Esteban had been evaluating the light of the conservatory without really thinking of it but now it came to the forefront of his mind. This, he said, may be the perfect sitting-room.

The baroness appeared puzzled for a moment . . . Oh, no, Herr Espíritu, I do not plan to sit for the portrait. I hardly want to be remembered to posterity as this dried-up old woman I've become. I want you to paint me in my youth, when I was a young woman who could turn heads.

Esteban was following her words intensely but wasn't certain he'd fully understood. You want me to paint a younger version of you. . . .

Yes, quite a lot younger in fact. Perhaps not so young as this—she touched the drawing of the gypsy girl—but it is the idea. The baroness continued after a brief pause, It appears you do not always require a live model but can also work from your fancy.

My fancy? . . .

Yes, your fancy—your imagination. But mind you, I want it to be accurate. I cannot protest my vanity but it has its limits. There is no need to render me a Venus.

I understand, said Esteban. Then you have some older portraits, some paintings or drawings, or perhaps a photograph or two, yes?

I sat for Herr de Guerre in Berlin, when I was traveling with my father the baron, but the Frenchman's solutions were apparently spoiled and nothing came of it. My husband the baron and I sat for a wedding portrait but before it was completed Stier entered into a disagreement with the artist and the painting was never finished—I'm quite certain the artist, who died many years ago, either destroyed the partially finished work or, more likely, reused the canvas and painted over it.

Esteban was quiet for a moment, translating, then: So there are no images from your youth, baroness?

No images at all, Herr Espíritu.

How then? . . .

The baroness raised a twig-like finger, knowing his question. She returned Esteban's work to him, and he placed it inside the case. On the table, she said, next to the golden-child orchid—and she gestured to her left.

Esteban stood and walked in the general direction until he saw a plant with brilliant yellow blooms and a table of dark walnut with legs carved in a Cornish style. The only objects on the table were a stack of four books, bound in well-worn black leather and tied as a single bundle by a red ribbon, and a statue of the Virgin Mary, held together by rusted wire as an obvious diagonal fissure ran between the Virgin's broken halves. The young painter picked up the books and returned to his chair.

My diaries, said the baroness, from the earliest years of my marriage. I was a devoted diarist then; I'm afraid I have fallen off in recent times.

Esteban held the books, which had a slightly musty odor, and examined them for a moment, confused: You want me to paint your portrait, to capture your likeness, accurately, by reading your diary entries from, sixty years ago. . . .

Quite so, Herr Espíritu, quite so.

I don't understand. . . .

Franz will visit you this evening with an advance so that you can purchase any supplies you may need. Perhaps you can come again, say, within the fortnight to share your ideas and any preliminary sketches.

Esteban thought that a breakdown in language accounted for the baroness's improbable request—that when he began examining the contents of the diaries it would all become clear. He managed to say, Of course.

Very good. There are some heavy canvas totes in the kitchen; please help yourself, for the diaries—the weather in the valley is quite unpredictable, especially this time of year.

Esteban thanked the baroness for the chocolate and excused himself with a slight bow. In Seville, the young always bowed to the aged, even regardless of their rank in society, and he hoped the custom was appropriate here as well.

In a few minutes he was back on the flagstone path, now doubly burdened for his return to the village. He thought he heard a distant growl of thunder.

FRAU BECKER, ESTEBAN'S LANDLADY, OPERATED A TAVERN OUT of her home's small summer-kitchen. In the afternoons, when he was finished with his work in the stables, Esteban would visit the tavern for a stein of stout beer and a pickled egg or two. He enjoyed listening to the old men argue about politics and reminisce regarding local history, their cigars and pipestems clenched between rotting teeth as they waved their stubby-fingered hands for emphasis. The conversations, though often meaningless to him in substance, assisted Esteban in learning the language, especially some of its more colorful phrases.

After his interview with the baroness, Esteban deposited his case and the diaries in his room, traded his olive jacket for his gray everyday one, and he went to Frau Becker's summer-kitchen. He was earlier than usual, and the regulars had not yet gathered. In fact Frau Becker wasn't even about, and everyone's absence made the space seem larger. In one corner a stand for the demikeg had been built from reused barnboards, and the stand mismatched perfectly the hodgepodge of stools, chairs and benches. It was a space purely of function with no consideration of form whatsoever. It smelled permanently of tobacco smoke and spilled beer, even with opposing windows thrown open to encourage a cross draft.

Through one window Esteban heard a horse and cart approach then stop. Even without seeing it, Esteban knew it was one of the workhorses of heavy breed, a Black Forester, they called it. He heard the powerful yet gentle creature shake the bells on his collar to signal the driver he was at full-stop and would remain so until instructed otherwise. Then Frau Becker, coming from the house's back porch, greeted the driver and said something about the beer of the previous week's shipment. Esteban heard no reply from the brewer's deliveryman.

In a moment the tavern door was pushed fully open and Frau Becker was backing into the summer-kitchen lugging a demikeg supported on the other end—to Esteban's surprise—by a quite pretty young girl, broad through the shoulders in spite of her thinness and as blond as winter wheat. Esteban immediately attempted to assist them but there was nothing for him to do, except stay out of their way.

Ah, our young man of Spain, Frau Becker wheezed in greeting as she and the girl wrestled their burden to the wall near the serving stand and sat it upon the plank floor as gently as they could manage.

May I help? said Esteban, trying not to stare into the molten sapphire of the girl's eyes, but not being wholly successful.

Yes, said his landlady, a woman as stout as the beer she served and whose deep-set laughter lines about her eyes and mouth added some angularity to her otherwise perfectly round face. She was no longer handsome but her expression at most times was pleasantly merry, even when doing hard work. Yes, Spain, she continued between puffing breaths, help Fräulein Hilde with . . . the remainder of the order. . . . Her father the brewmaster will . . . expect her home before dusk.

Esteban contentedly followed the brewmaster's daughter to the cart. She was tall, perhaps even an inch or more taller than Esteban. There was such a vivacious litheness to her body that even her loose-fitting blouse and long, patterned skirt could not conceal it.

There were a half dozen demikegs in the well-used cart, and the Black Forester was standing perfectly motionless, as if a still-life. Hilde seemed to read Esteban's thoughts:

Frau Becker receives two more.

Esteban nodded, then said: My name is not Spain, by the way—

I know—her gemstone eyes cutting him off as much as her voice—you are Esteban Espíritu, of Seville to be exact, and even though you are very good with horses your true passion is art. In fact you have only stopped here on your pilgrimage to the Rhine.

I see you know everything then.

You are famous, Señor Espíritu—we do not host many visitors, especially such . . .

Esteban hoped she would fill the space with a word for handsome or dashing . . .

. . . such exotic ones.

Hilde stepped up into the cart-bed. There is one thing I don't know, Señor, none of us do.

Esteban, please. What is that?

Why you have not moved on already.

I . . .

The Black Forester twitched his ears as if even he were interested in the response.

Hilde saved the young painter from the lingering absence of his answer by putting a demikeg on its side and rolling it to him with her foot, on which she wore a heavy shoe like any workman's. She was used to this sort of labor, as were all the villagers it seemed, and did not shrink from it.

In a few minutes they had carried the remainder of Frau Becker's order into the summer-kitchen; and Hilde had secured the other demikegs in the cart with thick leather straps. Esteban stood and watched, then waved to her as she sat in the cart-seat and shook the horse's reins to enliven him. She looked over at Esteban with her dangerous blue eyes one last time as the wheels began to move, but she and Esteban had said nothing further.

Come inside, Spain, called Frau Becker. The first stein and pickled egg are on the house. Besides, staring after the fräulein won't magically bring her back. The landlady cackled at Esteban's embarrassment.

He took up Frau Becker on her offer, and before long the quaint tavern was humming with its regular business. A pair of old men, Otto and Heinrich, had always been friendly to Esteban but on this evening they went further and invited him to occupy a stool in their usual corner. Otto, a former carpet dyer who lived with his daughter-in-law and adult grandson, was as bald as one of Frau Becker's pickled eggs and whistled a touch when he spoke due to a gap between his front teeth. Heinrich had three strapping sons who'd taken over the operation of his dairy farm, and also its large house with their wives and numerous children, leaving Heinrich to live on his own in the overseer's cottage. It was difficult for Esteban to picture little Heinrich's strapping sons, but the aged farmer's pure white hair and beard gave him the air of a biblical patriarch, so the young Sevillean accepted the sons' description as fact.

After a while of drinking and exchanging family histories—though Esteban had mainly confirmed what they already knew of him—Otto said, So they say you visited the witch today?

The witch . . . ?

Otto, don't be a rumor-monger, said Heinrich. He means the baroness. People here tell tales.

Yes, we had an interview.

Otto smiled. Her fellow, Franz, came to fetch you, did he?

Esteban felt a bit drunk, which didn't improve his translating skills. The very broad fellow, yes, he extended his mistress's invitation.

Otto snickered and his breath whistled between his teeth.

Esteban clearly was puzzled.

Don't mind him, said Heinrich, using his sleeve to dab beer from his snowy mustache. It is an old story: Franz, they say, became a resident of the baroness's household at the same time the old baron disappeared, well, died, in a boating accident in Switzerland—

There was no funeral, interrupted Otto, still grinning, only a private memorial.

Yes, the baron's body was never recovered, which isn't unusual in such cases.

So, said Esteban, trying to clear his head, would not the baroness require assistance after her husband's death? What is so strange about Franz entering into her employ?

Nothing, said Heinrich, nothing at all . . .

Except . . . said Otto.

Except?

Except, took up Heinrich, the suddenness of it—people seemed to recall that he arrived even before the news of the baron's demise.

So, what? said Esteban. She murdered her husband so she could bring this fat fellow into her house? Is that the gossip? He felt himself growing irritated with Otto and Heinrich, with the whole village.

Not precisely, whistled Otto. They say she and the baron argued, and she transformed him into this eunuch, Franz, and now the old baron does her bidding like a common servant.

Transformed him? Like placed him under a spell?

And that's not all—

Otto . . . cautioned his friend, though not very stridently.

Otto managed to maintain a mischievous grin while he gulped down some beer.

What? said Esteban impatiently.

Otto wiped his chin with his fingers. Well, they also say the baroness likes to transform herself into a young girl and come down to the village to, you know, spy on us . . . and what not.

It is a small village, said Esteban, would not a strange young girl showing up now and again raise some suspicions?

That is a good point, said hoary-headed Heinrich—but the gossips say she takes the form of a gypsy girl, and the gypsies are forever coming and going . . . who can keep track? But it's probably ridiculous.

A gypsy girl? Esteban stared at the old men, his head swimming—could they know about his sketches of the gypsy girl and be teasing him? He decided to play along: Now that I think of it, there was something familiar about the brewmaster's daughter, Hilde, whom I met earlier this evening.

The old men stopped drinking their beer and stared fixedly at Esteban. Otto said, The brewmaster's daughter? The brewmaster has no daughter; he is childless. . . .

Esteban looked at Heinrich but his expression remained blank . . . then both old men erupted in laughter.

We had you, didn't we, said Otto between snorts of whistling laughter. Wait until Fräulein Hilde hears the joke—she will love it; and Otto slapped Esteban on the shoulder.

Heinrich signaled Frau Becker to bring the pitcher and refill their steins.

The proprietress topped off their drinks, and the old men happily paid for Esteban's beer. The three sat for a moment listening to the din of the tavern patrons.

Then Otto said, So how did the baroness seem to you? She's not been down to the village in years, in a manner of speaking.

Esteban realized his ears were ringing. How did she seem?

Yes, you know, did she say or do anything strange?

Esteban thought of the baroness's diaries in his room. No, she was perfectly polite—nothing out of the ordinary. She merely wants me to paint her portrait, that is all.

Otto and Heinrich seemed to sense his lie but didn't press him. Esteban emptied his stein as quickly as he was able, thanked the pair for their generosity, then excused himself to his room. He did his best not to stagger from Frau Becker's crowded summer-kitchen.

Outside the cool night air instantly began to revive him. He looked for the moon and discovered that it was just rising above the baroness's house, which appeared pure black against the deeply violet sky.

3

In the predawn hour Esteban woke and recalled a fragment of the dream which he'd been having for months, since before leaving Seville even: A young man who is like Esteban but not him stalks the Minotaur in a labyrinth constructed of wooden chutes like the inner workings of the bullrings of Seville. Not-Esteban follows the Minotaur by sniffing his terrible stench and observing the trail of his enormous droppings. The eye of the labyrinth is like a bullring itself, and the Minotaur scratches at the patches of blood-soaked dust with his two cloven hooves, sweat dripping down his muscular shoulders and back, human in form except for their brown hide and gigantic beastly power. The Minotaur senses Not-Esteban's presence and begins to turn toward him. . . .

The dream always concluded before the young man sees the Minotaur's face.

At breakfast, which was fried mush topped with a soft-boiled egg and a strip of boiled pork, Esteban inquired with Frau Becker about the small corner room upstairs that appeared unoccupied—he wanted to paint there. They agreed on a price for two months' use. He then went to the stables but not to put in a day's labor. Rather, he used the baroness's generous advance to rent a horse and wagon, and he drove to the nearest town likely to have the materials he desired—quality canvases, the finest oil paints, vials of mineral and vegetable powders, stretching frames, a rock-solid easel, brushes tipped in ermine, cloths of Egyptian cotton, mortar and pestle of polished Venetian marble, linseed oil, and spirit of turpentine—the sorts of materials used only by the most celebrated masters.

Esteban underestimated the duration of the journey, and it

was long past midnight when he arrived back in the village. The moon had been obscured by clouds most of the night, rendering the roads all but invisible to Esteban, but the good horse he'd rented knew the way and had no trouble returning to his home. In fact, Esteban dozed during the final hour or two, thinking of the beautiful supplies he'd purchased, of sapphire-eyed Hilde, of Otto and Heinrich's wild stories, of Not-Esteban and the Minotaur. . . .

When he'd arrived, he unloaded the supplies as quietly as he could to Frau Becker's small parlor and returned the horse and wagon to their stable. By the time he'd properly cared for the trustworthy gelding and began to walk back to the boardinghouse, the eastern sky had begun its transformation to predawn indigo. He suspected his usual waking time was only an hour away. Today however he would sleep until noon.

The village was silent, save for the awakening chatter-song of birds; and the night air was at the depth of its chill before the coming sunrise. Though still on his feet, Esteban's exhausted mind began to drift into a kind of sleep state and again to images of the Minotaur at the center of his labyrinth. . . . Esteban was startled by the rusty groan of the gears of the village well, more or less in the center of the village's tiny square. In the earliest twilight Esteban's tired eyes discerned a female form at the well, turning the obstinate wheel to bring forth the subterranean water.

The litheness of the form's movements suggested she was youthful—and even in the low, blue-infused light he could discern the raven-wing hair past her shoulders and the peasant skirt and blouse of a gypsy. Was it the girl he'd drawn before at the well? He heard water begin to flow in the sluice.

Esteban, though not fifty paces from her and standing unshielded in the center of the empty street, had the sense that he was invisible, a true spirit whose boots hadn't even left impressions in the thoroughfare's gray dust.

The gypsy girl loosened the sluice's baffle and Esteban heard the water run into her wooden pail, which hung from a peg perfectly positioned to capture every drop. Meanwhile the twilight's indigo steadily faded to a deep lavender, showing more and more plainly the girl's slender form, and Esteban gazed with abandon as if she were modeling for him by choice. He gazed as if thirsty for the girl's pristine image.

She finished collecting water, closed the sluice's baffle, and hoisted the heavy pail by its thick handle of braided rope. She walked toward Esteban, who stood transfixed and began to believe he was indeed no more than a lingering night shadow falling across the lightening street. The girl was passing so close he smelled the strange spices that clung to her dark skin . . . but as she moved beyond him, she said, Good morning, Herr Painter—so softly Esteban thought perhaps he'd imagined it.

He gathered his jacket at his throat as a sudden chill ran through him. He turned and watched the girl's departing figure: she slipped between darkened buildings and was quickly out of sight. It comforted Esteban that she was walking in the direction of the gypsy encampment which, he knew, lay to the west of the village, in an area the locals called the Swamp.

4

By the time Esteban returned to Frau Becker's the landlady was in the kitchen preparing breakfast, and the scent of her strong Italian coffee filled the downstairs. It was enlivening to Esteban so instead of going directly to his room to sleep—a thought he'd been dwelling on for hours—he tapped on the open kitchen door, somewhat startling Frau Becker, who then prepared him a mug of coffee with thick, sweetened cream and sat him in a chair in the corner, cozily out of her way.

The landlady seemed to like the rare company and for more than an hour she chattered to him while she continued preparing her lodgers' breakfast. Urged by her pleasant questioning, Esteban told of his journey to the town and what it was like—when a newlywed, Frau Becker had often visited the town with her dairy farming husband, long deceased, and she enjoyed discovering how the town had changed and even more so how it had not. While they spoke Frau Becker had prepared another coffee for *Spain* and handed him a plate with buttermilk rolls, a poached egg, a boiled potato mashed with a fork and lightly peppered, and a chunk of beef brisket left over from dinner.

When the other lodgers began to come downstairs, Esteban went to his room. He looked at the plank bed with its straw-filled mattress, taking up a full third of the room, but he no longer felt sleepy. He removed his jacket and went to the small table in the corner, near the room's only window, sat in the solitary chair and untied the ribbon around the baroness's diaries, four in all. On the cover of each black volume was written in faded gold ink *K.L.* and the years, the earliest being *1866~67*.

Esteban began glancing through the diary, trying to become accustomed to the young baroness's handwriting. He opened the rose-tinted and rose-scented letter, which also lay on the table, and compared the thin, cursive scrawl to that on the diary pages. The baroness's hand had become weaker and less fluid over time but there was no question that the letter and the diary entries were penned by the same woman.

The diary took up in the first year of baroness Kristena's marriage to Stier von Lichtenberg, and the young bride, only seventeen, often wrote of the challenges of managing the household with its many servants and groundskeepers—even a huntsman was mentioned from time to time. The baron's social engagements seemed especially stressful to the girl whose parents were older when she was conceived and preferred their little family's quiet, close-knit company. It appeared the baron was quite exacting in his desires for their parties. One of their first rows was over a dress he wanted Kristena to wear . . .

It makes me appear a street trollop, too tight in the bodice and open at the throat besides.

The diary page was marred and some of the ink smeared suggesting that the girl baroness had shed tears over the ordeal. She wore the dress after all and one of the baron's guests, identified only as *J.*, had too much schnapps after dinner and drunkenly pawed Kristena throughout the evening. The baron seemed not to notice or care as long as his business ally was amused . . .

I was mauled like I was a common maid and he didn't so much as lift a finger or even raise an eyebrow at my distress. Just sat in the drawing room leering at J.'s daughter, a full year younger than I and stone-faced with wine, blinding herself to her father's deplorable behavior.

The diary entries returned to the mundane for several weeks—household matters and the weather, including a description of an evening when *moonlight shone through a shoal of fog rendering it a blue shroud which seemed to wrap around the entirety of the house*. Then the mundaneness was suddenly shattered on the sixteenth of June, 1866:

> *Does he think I'm a fool!—I know who the girl is, so does the entire staff no doubt, his gypsy whore, brought into the house as a scullery maid! Just to save him the trouble of having to go to the swamp to root around in her tent like swine . . . and to humiliate me.*

Perhaps it was the lack of sleep or the potent coffee, but Esteban felt as if he were slipping into the baroness's place, more than simply feeling sympathy for her unhappy marriage—rather, he felt her world upon his skin, tasted it upon his tongue.

Drunkenly overbearing one night, the baron tried to force himself into Kristena's bedchamber, irked by her aloofness to his concubine . . .

> *I would sooner die than have her filthy gypsy diseases brought into my bed. He pounded on the door cursing as if he intended to grant my wish.*

It was the girl who saved her. The baroness heard her, Zoria, coaxing the baron to their bed. At first it infuriated Kristena, calling her a wanton nymph, but even as she was writing the entry it came to her that Zoria was attempting to lure the baron away for her, the baroness's, sake—also that she and this girl were both captives here.—

A sound outside in the street, like heavy crates falling, broke Esteban's reverie and he was suddenly overcome with exhaustion. He put the baroness's scented letter in the diary to mark his place; then he rolled himself in a blanket on the bed and fell instantly asleep . . .

Not-Esteban is in the Minotaur's labyrinth, smelling his sweat, breathing in the humidity of his breath, which is the very air of the bullring's fetid passages. As he runs along, blind to a clear destination, Not-Esteban feels especially not himself. He experiences a kind of resigned pain, a familiar fear that over time has transformed into some other unnamed emotion. And even Not-Esteban's body moves in strange ways, quicker but less agile, perhaps taller yet definitely lighter. Not-Esteban puts out a hand to maintain balance, and skimming it along the rough boards of the chute a splinter penetrates the first finger—this is odd: in his dreams Esteban had never felt physical pain before. A bead of blood crimsons to the surface of the delicate-looking finger. Not-Esteban stares at the finger, intently watching as the bead drips from the wound and falls to the sandy floor. The blue muslin skirt and feminine shoes, between which the blood-drop lands, simultaneously elucidate and puzzle Not-Esteban: this dream-figure is a young woman, but who? The baroness Kristena? Zoria? They gypsy girl at the village well? Hilde, the brewmaster's daughter? The snort of the Minotaur, almost like the shout of a human voice, makes Not-Esteban look up, startled: he . . . she is in the eye of the bullring, and the beast has sensed her presence, perhaps smells the drop of blood, and he is turning his half human, half tauran head, the grotesque muscles of his back undulating beneath a sweaty sheen. Not-Esteban tries to become the Minotaur, to see with his sulfurous eyes. Instead, Not-Esteban thinks of Europa, ravaged by the bull. . . .

5

IT WAS NEARLY DARK WHEN ESTEBAN AWOKE. HE KNEW HE
had been thinking of the young baroness throughout his day-
time sleep, and over those many hours an image slowly formed
of her, like a picture emerging in the photographist's chemical
baths. She was a pretty but haunted figure, thin and pale, with
lustrous blond hair that saved her from seeming one of those
gothic heroines from the previous century's literature.

Esteban untangled himself from his blanket then lit the oil-
lamp in his room and retrieved his sketchbook and pencils. He
flipped past the gypsy drawings until he came to a clean sheet.
He searched the gallery of his memory for the familiar salon,
the one of the Minotaur dream, and found her there: the image of the young baroness. Esteban began with the thin line
of the left side of her face, wan and gaunt in his artist's eye,
and continued smoothly into her neck, then skimming across
to imply her clavicle, as fragile-looking as avian bones. The
pencil's charcoal tip briséd to the cleft of the youthful Kristena's
high bosom, surrounded by its plunging neckline, accented in
delicate Portuguese lace. The tip of Esteban's pencil traced the
opposite line of Kristena's neck, where dislodged strands of her
long hair looped and fell upon her bare shoulder. The pencil
worked on the baroness's ear, though mostly obscured by her
refulgent tresses.

And from this partial frame charcoal began to tease out
Kristena's distressed features, the thin arch of eyebrows, the
oval eyes with just the subtlest of Oriental angle, and wisps of
worry as light as a cob's solitary thread; the upturned nose with
its bridge's nearly invisible bump.

Finally his tip was at Kristena's lips. He took a moment to

sharpen his artist's instrument, which felt heavy with possibility between his graceful fingers. Then he placed the dark point at the corner of the young baroness's mouth and began by tracing her lower lip, plump with care—he knew her mouth would be key to the portrait, not the eyes, though they were a critical element as well. His pencil lingered at her lower lip for several minutes in an effort to render it perfectly, even on this first attempt.

When he began, lamplight and the final pulse of waning daylight cast the baroness's portrait in a citric wash; but now day had fully faded and the moon had crept into the sky opposite Esteban's lone window. Though weak, the gibbous added a touch of violet spectrum to his work emphasizing the baroness's mood of frustration and melancholy. Esteban used a smudging technique with the charcoal to highlight her cheekbones and to shadow her jawline and to round the crests of her bosom.

Then an element inserted itself into the sketch as if suggested by another. Esteban began drawing a hand flat against Kristena's stomach, just below her left breast. But he only rendered the most basic outline of the hand before stopping: he could not complete it because he knew not whose hand it was, not even if it were masculine or feminine.

6

DARKNESS HAD FALLEN LIKE A HEAVY BLUE CURTAIN BY THE time Esteban put away his materials, retied the diaries with the red ribbon, and straightened his rumpled bed. He thought of going to Frau Becker's summer-kitchen for beer but first he was drawn to peer out his window and on the street a figure was standing in a posture that suggested it was gazing up at his window. It was a feminine form and for a moment Esteban presumed it was the gypsy girl whom he'd seen at the well; however, just at that instant a horseman bearing a lantern trotted past the female form and the quick glint of light in her hair informed Esteban it was in fact the brewmaster's daughter, Hilde.

She seemed to raise her hand toward Esteban, who must have been an indistinct figure himself in the boardinghouse window. He took up his old jacket, locked his door from the hall, and hurried downstairs to meet her. Hilde was not in sight, though. He looked up and down the deserted street. Muffled conversations and punctuating laughter came from the summer-kitchen. A damp breeze blew his hair before his eyes; he had not cut his hair since leaving Seville and it had grown past his jacket collar. He pushed back his hair and as he did so he thought he glimpsed a figure in a blouse and long skirt pass between buildings down the street.

Esteban rushed to overtake the figure. He followed between the low brick buildings—one a small chapel, the other the village's post and telegraph office—and the figure had vanished again. The path led to the stable where he worked most regularly so it was perhaps out of habit that he continued in that direction even though there was no sign of the girl. As he neared the large, two-storey stable, the familiar smells of straw, oats, manure and equine sweat reached him on the chilling breeze.

When he reached the structure, he saw that one of its wide doors was ajar and saffron lamplight spilled angularly onto the ground. Though he did not mind being alone—he believed what his masters said, that true artists required their time of solitary contemplation—Esteban had had his fill today and felt the yearning for companionship. It seemed that one of the stable-hands or a groom was still at work—no one would leave a lamp burning unattended—so Esteban slipped through the barely open door.

Only two lamps were aglow, hanging from hooks on supporting timbers that ran along the wide central alley. To each side were occupied stalls (the horses seemed mildly unsettled), and at the midpoint of the alley crossed a narrow walkway that led to a tack-room and feed-room on one end and to an office with overnight quarters on the other.

Hello, called Esteban. Who is here?

There was no human response—the Forester to Esteban's right, the color of Frau Becker's sweetened coffee, dipped his enormous head and nickered softly at Esteban's voice.

Esteban advanced farther into the stable, becoming annoyed at the carelessness of leaving the lamps lit while stepping out for who knew what purpose. He tried to imagine which of the workers may have done it and three or four likely faces formed in his mind. He stood near the second burning lamp and watched while a serpent-shape of black smoke rose up from its glass chimney, an impurity in the oil, and it circled along the timber then vanished in the dark air of the rafters.

Espíritu

It was so quiet he thought his ears were deceiving him—that the casting of his name was only the whisper of the black smoke just before its serpent form fluttered to oblivion. Esteban peered up and down the central alley and into the stalls and up toward the railinged loft.

Espíritu

Esteban took the lamp from its hook and called, Who is there? Who is saying my name? He positioned the lamp to see farther into the nearby stalls—onyx eyes shone glossy from behind forelocks. He held the lamp higher, above his head, but the light could not penetrate the shadowed loft. He heard a subtle movement to his left that didn't strike him as quite equine, in the direction of the tack-room. Is someone there? He realized he'd only whispered the query, like a thespian on the stage. He began toward the tack-room, his lamp held before him as if an amulet. He'd only taken a few steps . . .

Herr Espíritu

. . . from behind and above, an androgynous voice lilting toward the feminine. Come down! You should not be up there! Footsteps as light as a child's scampered along the darkened creaking loft then after a moment ceased.

This prank is not funny . . . you could hurt yourself. . . .

Nothing—only the racing pulse in his ears and the horses' gentle movements behind their stall gates.

He thought that he should climb a ladder to the loft and put an end to the game-playing but he easily convinced himself the prankster had gone elsewhere. He decided instead to look in on each of the horses to make certain all were well. He'd been to several stalls and was stroking the neck of a powerful three-year-old named Hans when he spied a figure through an open upper gate in the back of the stall: the figure was all but invisible but seemed to be seated on the whitewashed corral fence and facing the yard and the stable.

Esteban's ire toward the brewmaster's daughter was extreme as he pushed open the door near the feed-room and marched toward the girl, his lamp still in hand and swinging light along the choppy ground. What do you think you are doing? Trying to frighten me with your childish game?

Hilde seemed startled, as if she'd been quite lost in her thoughts—What are you talking about? Childish game?

Yes, game!

Hilde's voice was strange. The girl finally fell within the weak arc of lamplight and it was not the brewmaster's daughter after all but rather the gypsy girl. Esteban stood before her speechless.

What game? she repeated after a few moments. The lamplight and moonlight competed to highlight her glossy ebon hair, which she'd loosed from her usual scarf so that it fell across her shoulders.

I thought you were someone else. . . .

So it would seem, Herr Painter. She turned about and leaped down from the fence's top rail and stood facing Esteban from the other side.

Were you in the stable?

When?

Just now?

Why would I be in the stable?

Esteban's flame wavered; from the weight of the lamp he'd known the font was nearly empty. Just a moment, I have to return the lantern. He began walking toward the stable door. Halfway he turned and called back, What is your name? The lamp went out altogether.

Zoria, she said, lost from view.

Esteban felt he was the butt of another joke . . . Zoria.

He quickly replaced the useless lamp, blew out the other, then exited and secured the streetside door. By the time he reached the opposite side of the stable, however, the girl was no longer by the fence; she seemed to be nowhere at all but in the utter darkness of a night shadow she may have only been steps away.

Esteban's yearning for companionship was even more intense and he felt drawn back toward the boardinghouse, believing it was the human-hive of the summer-kitchen he desired. However, as he was nearing Frau Becker's yard he heard the merry commotion and knew it didn't suit his mood and that it had not in fact been the object of his yearning. He went straight to his room, which now felt warm and a trifle stuffy, and he retrieved his sketchbook with the charcoal of young Kristena von Lichtenberg—it was as if he'd been missing her: not the living dowager but rather this rendering of her younger self, as totally false as it may be.

He placed the drawing on the table near the glowing lamp. He examined the mysterious hand beneath Kristena's breast and experienced a weird prick of jealousy. Though he had of course drawn the featureless hand himself it seemed even more of an enigma than before.

Esteban removed his jacket, raised the sash to let in some cooling air, then sat and prepared to draw further sketches of the young baroness. He began by untying the ribbon and reading from her diaries. Images of this flaxen-haired girl materialized in his mind's eye as if they'd been part of his hidden psyche all along and the diary entries were merely conjuring them forth, from shadow into light, that is, into the somber cerulean light which infused everything here.

Esteban read and sketched, the words firing his illustrative imagination: the girl baroness waltzing, the girl baroness wearing an expression of absence, the girl baroness weeping, the girl baroness writing, the girl baroness rising, the girl baroness writhing . . . all studies in the singular—except for the hand that inserted itself into every drawing: on the baroness's shoulder, on the baroness's hand, on her arm, her breast, her thigh.

He sketched through the night. In a corner of his window he absentmindedly noted the moon's rise and decline, at times obscured by wisps of lavender clouds drifting like dragon smoke across the picture-box sky.

7

FROM MY WINDOW, I WATCHED THE GIRL IN THE GARDEN AS SHE *carefully worked the weeding-hoe between rows of beets and lettuces and endive. It hasn't been an especially warm day, but she sweated through her white blouse, and she used a flowered scarf of scarlet to tie back her long black hair, trying to cool her glistening neck. I thought of how she no doubt sweats beneath the Baron's bulk—weeding must be a much more pleasurable way to raise one's perspiration . . . I rang for the downstairs maid, three times, but she was not answering the call, so I put on my dressing-gown and slippers, resolved to retrieve my own glass of buttermilk. It was not terribly late, not yet eleven, but the house was exceedingly quiet. For reasons that were not clear, I chose a longer route to the kitchen which took me past the Baron's private chambers; and just as I was there in the hallway, Stier's door opened—but before I had time to react I saw it was she, just as surprised as I but with the added emotion of shame. We stood facing one another and it burned in her tawny cheeks as clearly as if she'd handed me a missive of heartfelt apology. They say the eyes of gypsies are hypnotic—it aids in their mischief-making—and this Zoria's certainly were, such a deeply umberous brown they were nearly black. I sensed no mischief here, not of her making at least, and when she turned away to scurry down the hall, the breaking apart of our vision was almost physically painful . . . The music-room is at the end of the east hall, a hall otherwise of guestrooms and since we never invite overnight guests, the rooms are shut up and the furniture covered. No one has occupied the music-room for years, yet this morning—I had risen especially early—when I was passing the entrance to the east hall, I heard the faint notes of the piano, almost ghostly in their airiness. I stood in place for a* moment, but then there it was again—a mournful sound in the quiet, empty hall, made even more mournful by the badly out of tune instrument. I could not imagine who the pianist was—Stier did not play and had little appreciation for music anyway—and I thought again of the ghostliness of the sad melody. After hesitating a moment I proceeded down the hall, my velvet slippers light on the carpeted floor of red diamond pattern. As I drew closer to the music-room I knew the piece, the 'Lovers' Sonata' by Schlönberg, but I'd never heard it played so adagio, so melancholy. I hesitated at the door, which was half ajar. Perhaps the pianist wanted his privacy? Perhaps I could satisfy my curiosity without disturbing his playing. I carefully pushed back the door just far enough to take a single step into the room and observe the piano and its player—I was quite shocked to see the girl, Zoria, on the embroidered bench. She wore a silk robe of deepest scarlet and her face was hooded by her dark untethered hair. She was quite focused on the sheets of music and as such lost in the moment, affording me to watch her in profile for some time while the bittersweet notes fell upon the still air. On a small table near the piano was a statuette of the Virgin, blue-cloaked and beatific, the only art in the somber and colorless music-room. I quietly stepped back into the hall, not wishing to disturb the girl, nor to be discovered watching and listening so intensely . . . Another night of fitful sleeping, dreamt again of performing a duet with the girl—we are in a large concert hall, the houselights have been turned down, it seems that every seat is occupied but the audience's faces are obscured, I wonder if the Baron is in attendance, perhaps seething with jealousy, then I know he is not, and our playing takes on a lightness in the perfectly acoustical hall. . . .

8

IT WAS THE COMMOTION IN THE HALL WHICH FIRST WOKE Esteban, Frau Becker having words with someone, and Esteban was thinking he should get out of bed to see what was happening when there was pounding on his door. He rose so quickly his head swam as he surveyed the messy room for his pants—sketches lay on the table, the floor, even the foot of his bed, and the baroness's diaries were open here and there—

More knocking and a man's angry voice: Open the door, Spaniard!

Still disoriented, Esteban realized he was wearing his pants, that he'd only managed off his heavy canvas shirt before crawling into sleep. Sí, sí—I mean, yes, just a moment; and he opened the door.

An enormous blond fellow filled the door frame, blond hair, blond beard. Where is she?

I'm sorry, Spain—Frau Becker spoke from behind the flush-cheeked fellow—I asked him to wait in the parlor . . .

Where is she? And he began surveying Esteban's disheveled room.

Frau Becker, now peeping from a small space between the fellow's meaty biceps muscle and the frame, spoke again: This is Herr Müeller, the brewmaster . . .

Finally some clarity came to Esteban—Ah, you are looking for your daughter . . .

Of course, what did you think, Spaniard, I'd come to invite you to drink a beer with me! Where is my Hilde?

I do not know where the fräulein is. I have not been with her.

Herr Müeller's frosty eyes darted about the tiny, unkempt

room as if seeking a place where his daughter may be hiding, though obviously an impossibility. But you know where she is . . .

No, said Esteban, suddenly realizing it was a lie, or nearly so—he somehow did sense where Fräulein Hilde may be keeping herself—but he merely reiterated: I thought perhaps I had seen her on the street, from my window (he peered over his shoulder for a second at the window, as if to prove the veracity of his statement) but I have not spoken to her since our brief introduction at Frau Becker's.

Two days ago, offered the landlady, invisibly. Perhaps Hilde is only taking a stroll in the woods.

Dissatisfied, Herr Müeller stormed off, headstrong as a bull to locate his overdue daughter.

Frau Becker and Esteban looked at each other for a moment; then she noticed the condition of his room. Yet she merely said, The coffee is ready—I will fry you a blintz with potato and egg.

Thank you; I will be downstairs in a moment.

Esteban dressed and ate quickly, so it was only a matter of minutes after the brewmaster's visit that Esteban was on the road leading to the gypsy encampment, the whereabouts of which he knew only by reputation.

It was becoming an overcast day with a threat of rain on the azure air. A mile or more beyond the boundaries of the village the road began to slope downward, and in a few minutes a well-trod path appeared falling away from this already secondary road—the deep ruts of cart-wheels and mule hooves showed Esteban he was on the correct course. He thought of the gypsies, of Zoria in particular, carrying well water such a great distance: Shiftless, the villagers said, but there was no doubting the gypsies' heartiness. The quality of the air had changed and was suddenly tinged with a fenny dankness. But there were also the scents of cookfires and the sweat of mules, and Esteban soon came to the camp of tents and carts and flimsy moveable shacks.

Besides the mules, which were tethered to posts or stumps here and there, Esteban noted molting chickens, splay-legged goats, halfbreed herding dogs, and a trio of undernourished milk cows—in fact, at first look it appeared a camp solely of animals. Shouldn't there also be music-playing monkeys, chained tigers and dancing bears? In a moment Esteban was approached by a short fellow with black mustaches, twisted at their ends, and shoulders as broad as a water yoke. He'd been carving a block of pine, and the wood and knife were still in hand.

May I help you?—his German almost as poorly accented as Esteban's.

I am looking for my friend, Zoria—calling her a friend didn't feel like a lie.

The broad little fellow studied Esteban's face suspiciously, all the while turning the handle of the knife over in his large, heavily creased palm. Esteban saw that he was carving an animal shape in the block of pine—it appeared to be a bull rearing on his hind legs, which were yet undefined in the wood. Meanwhile other gypsies had emerged from their tents and shacks and were looking at Esteban warily.

The long moment was broken by a feminine voice: Herr Painter—what are you doing here?

Esteban turned to her, still half hidden by a tent flap: Your father is looking for you, Fräulein Müeller.

The black-haired girl Zoria appeared next to Hilde in the tent's opening.

Hilde said, Did you tell him of your suspicions?

Esteban shook his head. I did not.

Zoria said, We were about to have breakfast, Herr Painter—join us. Then she spoke to her people in their own tongue and they returned to whatever they'd been doing beforehand.

The young women, both in simple blouses and flowered

skirts that reached to their unshod feet, led Esteban through the ramshackle camp without speaking. He was somewhat behind and able to observe them unabashedly—he was reminded of a printed photograph and the photographist's glass-plate negative image, the girls were so similar in height and form and even gracefulness, and only varied greatly in their lightness and darkness.

They came to a part of the camp set up for dining, where two large copper pots were suspended above smoking fires, and at a third fire meat was sizzling in an enormous iron pan. There was also an odd assortment of chairs, stools, tables but also stumps and rough-hewn logs, around which here and there were a few old men and children—while a trio of thickbodied women appeared to be in charge of preparing and serving the meal.

Esteban, Hilde and Zoria seated themselves at a round table, and in a moment they were served bowls of thick porridge with, Esteban discovered, bits of meat (goat, he assumed) and a strong scent of sage. He was also given a cup of milk, still warm from the udder. The woman who served them set a fourth place, and when she brought the small pail of milk she seated herself. Her complexion was darker than Zoria's and uneven with darker still age spots from long hours working out of doors; her hair was bound in a purple scarf but Esteban noted filaments of white mixed with the ebon strands which had come loose. She was perhaps forty or forty-five, the age of his mother back in Seville.

For a time they ate in silence with their wooden spoons while around them old men and children chattered amongst themselves in the language Esteban couldn't identify.

When they were nearly finished with their food, an old woman came holding a metal coffee pot with a rag, steam rising from its spout, and she poured the richly black coffee into the cups which had held their milk. The woman at their table removed pouch and paper from a pocket of her skirt and deftly rolled a cigarette, then stuck a match on the underside of the table to light it. The smoke escaped her lips as she spoke: Now we can talk—her German was perfect. It is funny, Herr Painter, but the question you keep raising around you is, Why is he here? The village folk ask it because they believed you had designs to move on months ago. The stable operators ask it because you are so gifted with horses that it seems a waste for you to be tending simple beasts of burden. And now here you are, in our home, and we find ourselves asking it too. She brought the cigarette to her lips as she finished speaking.

I did not realize, said Esteban, I was such a source of wonderment.

The woman studied him with brown eyes flecked in blue, and she didn't need to comment that his response was equivalent to no response at all.

Then he said, The light. . . .

The light?

Yes, there is something about it—I cannot say that it drew me here—

Like a moth to a flame, offered the woman.

But once I saw it . . . well, it seems to have cast a spell upon me, or something to that effect.

It is blue, the light.

Yes, yes, quite so—you see it too.

How can one not?

Sapphire-eyed Hilde spoke up: Blue is the color of sorrow.

And of fidelity, said Zoria as a counterpoint.

And of nobility, said the woman, more smoke rising from her lips.

Here, said Esteban, I am afraid it is mainly the color of sorrow.

Don't be so certain, Herr Painter—it is safe to say that blue is a complex color and not easily known.

Esteban drank the rich coffee. Then: I could ask the same

of you.

The woman arched her black eyebrows in puzzlement.

Why are you here? You are nomads, yes? Why not move elsewhere, someplace where the air is less . . . oppressive?

Perhaps we are.

You are planning to move on?

No, perhaps we are moving now, even as you and I speak, but at such an incremental pace it is impossible to detect in the short term. Like a glacier.

Perhaps I too am traveling to the Rhine at the same rate. Like a glacier.

Perhaps, said the woman, and she touched her cup to Esteban's in confederation.

Large drops of rain began to fall noisily upon the table top, and everyone in the camp started to seek shelter, including the woman and the two girls. Esteban rose from the table—there was more he wanted to say, to know . . .

He followed the woman as she was hurrying off, and he reached out and touched her shoulder.

She stopped and turned, tossing away what little was left of her cigarette and then using her hand to shield her face from the raindrops, which were falling faster now.

Esteban said, Something happened . . .

Where? When?

At the baroness's house . . . something bad. His German was failing him in the rush of the moment.

The woman looked at him for a second or two: Something bad, Herr Painter, or something . . . complex? Then she turned and went quickly into a nearby tent. Farther away, Zoria and Hilde, holding hands, also disappeared behind a tent's flapped opening.

No one invited Esteban in to shelter from the rain. The wind also had risen. He pulled the collar of his jacket over his head, thinking, What *am* I doing here?

BY THE TIME ESTEBAN REACHED FRAU BECKER'S HE WAS SOAK-
ed completely, and waves of chill cascaded through his body
like electric current, which he'd once seen demonstrated in the
capital. He went directly to his room, meaning to swiftly shed
his wet clothes and wrap himself in blankets, but upon entering
his room he saw that it had been tidied—no doubt by his landlady—and she'd even neatly pinned his sketches to the walls.
The baroness's diaries were reassembled, bound together with
the red ribbon, and placed on the table along with his sketchbook, pencils and sharpening stone.

I hope you don't mind, Spain.

He was standing in the open doorway to his room, and Frau
Becker was behind him in the hall.

No, it is fine, said Esteban, a shiver accenting the word *fine*.

Give me your wet things and I'll dry them in the parlor. I'll
also bring you hot chocolate with gingerbread—it'll ward off
lung fever.

Presently, Esteban had changed into his dry clothing, and
with a blanket around his shoulders he was looking at his
sketches in the gray-blue light from the window. Frau Becker
tapped on the door and entered with the steaming chocolate
and a thick slice of gingerbread, both of which she placed on
the table next to Esteban.

Then she joined him in gazing at the drawings.

There seemed to be an order to them, she said, almost like
they're telling a story.

After a moment Esteban said, Did you know Baroness von
Lichtenberg when she was younger?

Not really, my husband and I were on the farm until, what,

twelve years ago, but I knew of her of course. And of the baron's accident.

His drowning.

Yes, the baron's drowning.

Esteban waited for her to elaborate, to express her skepticism, but she didn't share Heinrich and Otto's fondness for gossip, and only the landlady's tone possibly hinted at something untoward.

Drink your chocolate while it is hot, Spain, and eat the gingerbread whether you care for it or not. I have no desire to nurse a sick lodger—that's not part of our arrangement. Frau Becker smiled and left Esteban alone.

He did what he was instructed, and the food and drink did assist in warming him further. Nevertheless he went to his bed and burrowed beneath the extra blankets Frau Becker had brought him. Rain pelted his window, and in a moment he had returned to the Minotaur's labyrinth as the female figure he knew to be the young Kristena . . .

She is following the beast's scent, treading upon the sandy floor as lightly as she is able. The passageway is in severe shadow but she resists lighting a lamp though they appear now and then on the rough-plank walls. Surprise is her ally—that and Mother Mary, whose graceful beads she holds in her palm, rubbing gently with her thumb and fingers. The motion releases a scent like lilac and it helps to mask the beast's semi-human stench. She reaches the entrance and steps quietly into the eye of the labyrinth. She hears the beast's grunts before spying him in the dim light—there in the center of his world, taking the girl, sweat rolling off his bestial shanks with every brutish thrust. As silent as fate, she goes to the beast, oblivious in his copulation, and she raises the beads above her head . . . at that moment her prayers are answered in the form of the Virgin herself, which she brings unto the beast's skull with the full force of her divinity. . . .

The day was still rainy when Esteban awoke, and immediately he began the task of completing the feminine details of the hand in his sketches. When the weather cleared, he would gather his work and begin the long climb to the baroness's lonely house, beneath a sky of piercing blue.

www.ingramcontent.com/pod-product-compliance
Lightning Source LLC
Chambersburg PA
CBHW030328130626
46554CB00011B/1052